Cont

GW00994416

Guess

That last day of October a freak storm hit the suburb of Woodley Park. Slates rattled off roofs, dustbins chased dustbin lids along the streets, hoardings were slammed down, and at midnight there was a huge sound like a giant breaking his kindling wood, and then an almighty crash, and then briefly the sound of the same giant crunching his toast.

Then only the wind, which died surprisingly soon.

In the morning everyone could see that the last forest tree of Grove Road – of the whole suburb – had fallen, crashing down on to Grove Road Primary School. No lives had been lost, since the caretaker did not live on the premises; but the school hamster had later to be treated for shock. The school buildings were wrecked.

Everyone went to stare, especially, of course, the children of the school. They included Netty and Sid Barr.

The fallen tree was an awesome sight, partly because of its size and partly because of its evident great age. Someone in the crowd said that the acorn that grew into *that* must have been planted centuries ago.

As well as the confusion of fallen timber on the road and on the school premises, there was an extraordinary spatter of school everywhere: slates off the roof, bricks from the broken walls, glass from the windows, and the contents of classrooms, cloakrooms and storerooms – books and collages and clay and paints and Nature tables and a queer mixture of clothing, both dingy and weird, which meant that the contents of the Lost Property cupboard and the dressing-up cupboard had been whirled together and tossed outside. Any passer-by could have taken his pick, free of charge. Netty Barr, who had been meaning to claim her gym-shoes from Lost Property, decided that they had gone for good now. This was like the end of the world – a school world.

Council workmen arrived with gear to cut, saw and haul timber. Fat old Mr Brown from the end of the Barrs' road told the foreman that they ought to have taken the tree down long ago. Perhaps he was right. In spite of last season's leaves and next year's buds, the trunk of the tree was quite hollow: a cross-section revealed a rim of wood the width of a man's hand, encircling a space large enough for a child or smallish

adult. As soon as the workmen's backs were turned, Sid Barr crept in. He then managed to get stuck and had to be pulled out by Netty. An untidy young woman near by was convulsed with silent laughter at the incident.

"You didn't stay inside for a hundred years," she said to Sid.

"That smelt funny," said Sid. "Rotty." Netty banged his clothes for him: the smell clung.

"Remember that day last summer, Net? After the picnic? When I got stuck inside the great old tree in Epping Forest?" Sid liked to recall near-disasters.

"Epping Forest?" said the young woman, sharply interested. But no one else was.

Meanwhile the headmaster had arrived, and that meant all fun was over. School would go on, after all, even if not in these school-buildings for the time being. The pupils of Grove Road were marshalled and then sent off in groups to various other schools in the neighbourhood. Netty and Sid Barr, with others, went to Stokeside School: Netty in the top class, Sid in a lower one.

There was a good deal of upheaval in Netty's new classroom before everyone had somewhere to sit. Netty was the next-to-last to find a place; the last was a thin, pale girl who chose to sit next to Netty. Netty assumed that she was a Stokesider; yet there was something familiar about her, too. Perhaps she'd just seen her about. The girl had dark, lank hair gathered into a pony-tail of sorts, and a pale pointed face with greyish-green eyes. She wore a dingy green dress that looked ready for a jumble sale, and gym-shoes.

Netty studied her sideways. At last, "You been at Stokeside long?" Netty asked.

The other girl shook her head and glanced at the teacher, who was talking. She didn't seem to want to talk; but Netty did.

"A tree fell on our school," whispered Netty. The other girl laughed silently, although Netty could see nothing to laugh about. She did see something, however: this girl bore a striking resemblance to the young woman who had watched Sid being pulled from the hollow tree-trunk. The silent laughter clinched the resemblance.

Of course, this girl was much, much younger. Of course.

"How old are you?" whispered Netty.

The girl said a monosyllable, still looking amused.

"What did you say?"

Clearly now: "Guess."

Netty was furious: "I'm just eleven," she said coldly.

"So am I," said the other girl.

Netty felt tempted to say "Liar"; but instead she asked, "Have you an elder sister?"

"No."

"What's your name?"

Again that irritating monosyllable. Netty refused to acknowledge it. "Did you say Jess?" she asked.

"Yes. Jess."

In spite of what she felt, Netty decided not to argue about that Jess, but went on: "Jess what?"

The girl looked blank.

"I'm Netty Barr; you're Jess Something – Jess what?"

This time they were getting somewhere: after a tiny hesitation, the girl said, "Oakes."

"Jess Oakes. Jessy Oakes." But whichever way you said it, Netty decided, it didn't sound quite right; and that was because Jess Oakes herself didn't seem quite right. Netty wished now that she weren't sitting next to her.

At playtime Netty went out in the playground; Jess Oakes followed her closely. Netty didn't like that. Unmistakably, Jess Oakes wanted to stick with her. Why? She hadn't wanted to answer Netty's questions; she hadn't been really friendly. But she clung to Netty. Netty didn't like it – didn't like *her*.

Netty managed to shake Jess Oakes off, but then saw her talking with Sid on the other side of the playground. That made her uneasy. But Jess Oakes did not reappear in the classroom after playtime: Netty felt relieved, although she wondered. The teacher made no remark.

Netty went cheerfully home to tea, a little after Sid.

And there was Jess Oakes sitting with Sid in front of the television set. Netty went into the kitchen, to her mother.

"Here you are," said Mrs Barr. "You can take all the teas in." She was loading a tray.

"When did *she* come?" asked Netty.

"With Sid. Sid said she was your friend." Netty said nothing. "She's a lot older than you are, Netty."

"She's exactly my age. So she says."

"Well, I suppose with that face and that figure – or that no-figure – she could be any age. Any age."

"Yes."

Mrs Barr looked thoughtfully at Netty, put down the bread knife she still held, and with decision set her hands on her hips: "Netty!"

"Yes?"

"I don't care what age she is, I like your friends better washed than that."

Netty gaped at her mother.

"She smells," said Mrs Barr. "I don't say it's unwashed body, I don't say it's unwashed clothes – although I don't think much of hers. All I know is she smells nasty."

"Rotty," said Netty under her breath.

"Don't bring her again," said Mrs Barr crisply.

Netty took the tea-tray in to the other two. In the semi-dark they all munched and sipped while they watched the TV serial. But Netty was watching Jess Oakes: the girl only seemed to munch and sip: she ate nothing, drank nothing.

A friend called for Sid, and he went out. Mrs Barr looked in to ask if the girls wanted more tea: Netty said no. When her mother had gone, Netty turned off the television and switched on the light. She faced Jess Oakes: "What do you want?"

The girl's green glance slid away from Netty. "No harm. To know something."

"What?"

"The way home."

Netty did not ask where she had been living, or why she was lost, or any other commonsense questions. They weren't the right questions, she knew. She just said savagely: "I wish I knew what was going on inside your head, Jess Oakes."

Jess Oakes laughed almost aloud, as though Netty had said

something really amusing. She reached out her hand and touched Netty, for the first time: her touch was cool, damp.

"You shall," she said. "You shall."

And where was Netty now? If she were asleep and dreaming, the falling asleep had been very sudden, at the merest touch of a cool, damp hand. But certainly Netty must be dreaming...

She dreamt that she was in a strange room filled with a greenish light that seemed partly to come in through two windows, of curious shape, set together rather low down at one side. The walls and ceilings of this chamber were continuous, as in a dome; all curved. There was nothing inside the dome-shaped chamber except the greenish light, of

a curious intensity; and Netty. For some reason Netty wanted to look out of the two windows, but she knew that before she could do that, something was required of her. In her dreaming state, she was not at first sure what this was, except that it was tall – very tall – and green. Of course, green: green in spring and summer, and softly singing to itself with leaves; in autumn, yellow and brown and red, and its leaves falling. In winter, leafless. A tree, a forest tree, a tree of the Forest, a tree of Epping Forest. A tree – a hundred trees – a thousand trees – a choice of all the trees of Epping Forest. She had been to the Forest; she was older than Sid, and therefore she knew the direction in which the Forest lay, the direction in which one would have to go to reach the Forest. Her knowledge of the Forest and its whereabouts was in the green-glowing room, and it passed from her in that room, and became someone else's knowledge too...

Now Netty knew that she was free to look out of the windows of the room. The frames were curiously curved; there was not glass in them, but some other greenish-grey substance. She approached the windows; she looked through them, and she saw into the Barrs' sitting-room, and she saw Netty Barr sitting in her chair by the television set, huddled in sudden sleep.

She saw herself apart from herself, and she cried out in terror, so that she woke, and she was sitting in her chair, and the girl who called herself Jess Oakes was staring at her with her grey-green eyes, smiling.

"Thank you," said Jess Oakes. "Now I know all I need to know." She got up, unmistakably to go. "Good-bye."

She went out of the sitting-room, leaving the door open; Netty heard her go out of the front door, leaving that open too. The doors began to bang in a wind that had risen. The front gate banged as well.

Mrs Barr came crossly out of the kitchen to complain. She saw that Netty was alone in the sitting-room. "Has she gone, then?"

Netty nodded, dumb.

They went into the hall together. Scattered along the hall were pieces of clothing: one gym-shoe by the sitting-room door, another by the coat-hooks; a dingy green dress, looking like something out of a dressing-up box, by the open front door...

Mrs Barr ran to the front gate and looked up and down the road. No one; just old Mr Brown on the lookout, as usual. Mrs Barr called to him: "Have you seen anyone?"

"No. Who should I have seen?"

Mrs Barr came back, shaken. "She can't have gone stark naked," she said. Then, as an afterthought, "She can't have gone, anyway." Then again, "But she has gone."

Netty was looking at the gym-shoes in the hall. She could see inside one of them; and she could see a name printed there. It would not be JESS OAKES; it would be some other name. Now she would find out the true identity of the girl with the greenish eyes. She stooped, picked up the shoe, read the name: NETTY BARR.

"Those are the gym-shoes you lost at school," said Mrs Barr. "How did she get hold of them? Why was she wearing them? What kind of a girl or a woman was she, with that smell on her? Where did she come from? And where's she gone? Netty, you bad girl, what kind of a friend was she?"

"She wasn't my friend," said Netty.

"What was she then? And where's she gone – *where's she gone?*"

"I don't know," said Netty. "But guess."

Tomoko's letter

1552-1 C

Fujin

April, 15, 1

My Dear Friend,

I would be very glad to a exchange letters with you. Now I will tell you something about my self. I am a girl named Tomoko Kawarasaki (Tomo=Friend=とも, ko=child=こ) I am to be 18, August 17. In my family there are six, my mother and father, my big sister and little brother, my grandmother. I have a big sister who is 18. Her named is Takako. Takako goes to Showajoshi' University in Tokyo. I also have a little brother. His name is Toru. and he is elementary school the sixth.

By the way, my nick name is Tonbe and Tomochan. I like music. (I like playing the flute......). I go to Fujinomiyanishi' High School and I'm the first grade.

The climate is pretty mild in Japan. This is spring, so the weather is very beautiful. Most of the flowers are in bloom and the leaves are starting to come out. How is the weather in England? Which season of the year do you like best?

I like to see the baseball. but, I don't like to sports.

Please send me a picture of yourself.

It is getting late, so I must be saying good-by for now and will be waiting to hear from you again.

Yours truly
Tomoko Kawarasaki

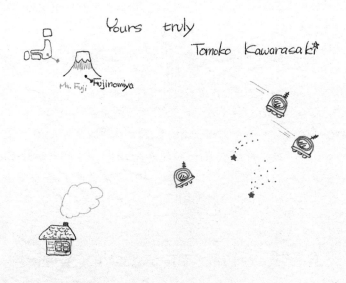

Mt. Fuji Fujinomiya

Lenny's red-letter day

Lenny Fraser is a boy in my class. Well, he's a boy in my class when he comes. But to tell the truth, he doesn't come very often. He stays away from school for a week at a time, and I'll tell you where he is. He's at the shops, stealing things sometimes, but mainly just opening the doors for people. He does it to keep himself warm. I've seen him in our shop. When he opens the door for someone, he stands around inside till he gets sent out. Of course, it's quite warm enough in school, but he hates coming. He's always got long, tangled hair, not very clean, and his clothes are too big or too small, and they call him "Flea-bag". He sits at a desk without a partner, and no one wants to hold his hand in games. All right, they're not to blame; but he isn't, either. His mother never gets up in the morning, and his house is dirty. It's a house that everybody runs past very quickly.

But Lenny makes me laugh a lot. In the playground he's always saying funny things out of the corner of his mouth. He doesn't smile when he does it. He says these funny things as if he's complaining. For example, when Mr Cox the deputy head came to school in his new car, Lenny came too, that day; but he didn't join in all the admiration. He looked at the little car and said to me, "Anyone missing a skateboard?"

He misses all the really good things, though – the School Journeys and the outing. And it was a big shame about his birthday.

It happens like this with birthdays in our class. Miss Blake lets everyone bring their cards and perhaps a small present to show the others. Then everyone sings "Happy Birthday" and we give them bumps in the playground. If people can't bring a present, they tell everyone what they've got instead. I happen to know some people make up the things that they've got just to be up with the others, but Miss Blake says it's good to share our Red-Letter Days.

I didn't know about these Red-Letter Days before. I thought they were something special in the post, like my dad handles in his Post Office in the shop. But Miss Blake told us they are red printed words in the prayer books, meaning special days.

Well, what I'm telling you is that Lenny came to school on his birthday this year. Of course, he didn't tell us it was his birthday, and, as it all worked out, it would have been better if Miss Blake hadn't noticed in the register. But, "How nice!" she said. "Lenny's here on his birthday, and we can share it with him."

It wasn't very nice for Lenny. He didn't have any cards to show the class, and he couldn't think of a birthday present to tell us about. He couldn't even think of anything funny to say out of the corner of his mouth. He just had to stand there looking foolish until Miss Blake started the singing of "Happy Birthday" – and then half the people didn't bother to sing it. I felt very sorry for him, I can tell you. But that wasn't the worst. The worst happened in the playground. I went to take his head end for bumps, and no one would come and take his feet. They all walked away. I had to finish up just patting him on the head with my hands, and before I knew what was coming out I was telling him, "You can come home to tea with me, for your birthday." And he said, yes, he would come.

My father works very hard in the Post Office, in a corner of our shop; and my mother stands at the door all day, where people pay for their groceries. When I get home from school, I carry cardboard boxes out to the yard and jump on them, or my big sister Nalini shows me which shelves to fill and I fill them with jam or chapattis – or birthday cards. On this day, though, I thought I'd use my key and go in through the side door and take Lenny straight upstairs – then hurry down again and tell my mum and dad that I'd got a friend in for an hour. I thought, I can get a birthday card and some cake and ice-cream from the shop, and Lenny can go home before they come upstairs. I wanted him to do that before my dad saw who it was, because he knows Lenny from his hanging around the shops.

Lenny said some funny things on the way home from school, but you know, I couldn't relax and enjoy them properly. I felt ashamed because I was wishing all the time that I hadn't asked him to come home with me. The bottoms of his trousers dragged along the ground, he had no buttons on his shirt so the sleeves flapped, and his hair must have made it hard for him to see where he was going.

I was in luck because the shop was very busy. My dad had a queue of people to pay out, and my mum had a crowd at the till. I left Lenny in the living-room and I went down to get what I wanted from the shop. I found him a birthday card with a badge in it. When I came back, he was sitting in a chair and the television was switched on. He's a good one at helping himself, I thought. We watched some cartoons and then we played "Monopoly", which Lenny had seen on the shelf. We had some crisps and cakes and lemonade while we were playing; but I had only one eye on my "Monopoly" moves – the other eye was on the clock all the time. I was getting very impatient for the game to finish, because it looked as if Lenny would still be there when they came up from the shop. I did some really bad moves so that I could lose quickly, but it's very difficult to hurry up "Monopoly", as you may know.

In the end I did such stupid things – like buying too many houses and selling Park Lane and Mayfair – that he won the game. He must have noticed what I was doing, but he didn't say anything to me. Hurriedly, I gave him his birthday card. He pretended not to take very much notice of it, but he put it in his shirt, and kept feeling it to make sure it was still there. At least, that's what I thought he was making sure about, there inside his shirt.

It was just the right time to say goodbye, and I'm just thinking he can go without anyone seeing him, when my sister came in. She had run up from the shop for something or other, and she put her head inside the room. At some other time, I would have laughed out loud at her stupid face. When she saw Lenny, she looked as if she'd opened the door and seen something really unpleasant. I could gladly have given her a good kick. She shut the door a lot quicker than she opened it, and I felt really bad about it.

"Nice to meet you," Lenny joked, but his face said he wanted to go, too, and I wasn't going to be the one to stop him.

I let him out, and I heaved a big sigh. I felt good about being kind to him, the way you do when you've done a sponsored swim, and I'd done it without my mum and dad frowning at me about who I brought home. Only Nalini had seen him, and everyone knows she can make things seem worse than they are. I washed the glasses, and I can remember singing while I stood at the sink. I was feeling very pleased with myself.

My good feeling lasted about fifteen minutes; just long enough to be wearing off slightly. Then Nalini came in again and destroyed it altogether.

"Prakash, have you seen that envelope that was on the television top?" she asked. "I put it on here when I came in from school."

"No," I said. It was very soon to be getting worried, but things inside me were turning over like clothes in a washing-machine. I knew already where all this was going to end up. "What was in it?" My voice sounded to me as if it was coming from a great distance.

She was looking everywhere in the room, but she kept coming back to the television top as if the envelope would mysteriously appear there. She stood there now, staring at me. "*What was in it?* What was in it was only a Postal Order for five pounds! Money for my school trip!"

"What does it look like?" I asked, but I think we both knew that I was only stalling. We both knew where it had gone.

"It's a white piece of paper in a brown envelope. It says 'Postal Order' on it, in red."

My washing-machine inside nearly went into a fast spin when I heard that. It was certainly Lenny's Red-Letter Day! But how could he be so ungrateful, I thought, when I was the only one to be kind to him? I clenched my fist while I pretended to look around. I wanted to punch him hard on the nose.

Then Nalini said what was in both our minds. "It's that

dirty kid who's got it. I'm going down to tell Dad. I don't know what makes you so stupid."

Right at that moment I didn't know what made me so stupid, either, as to leave him up there on his own. I should have known. Didn't Miss Banks once say something about leopards never changing their spots?

When the shop closed, there was an awful business in the room. My dad was shouting-angry at me, and my mum couldn't think of anything good to say.

"You know where this boy lives," my dad said. "Tell me now, while I telephone the police. There's only one way of dealing with this sort of thing. If I go up there, I shall only get a mouthful of abuse. As if it isn't bad enough for you to see me losing things out of the shop, you have to bring untrustworthy people upstairs!"

My mum saw how unhappy I was, and she tried to make things better. "Can't you cancel the Postal Order?" she asked him.

"Of course not. Even if he hasn't had the time to cash it somewhere else by now, how long do you think the Post Office would let me be Sub-Postmaster if I did that sort of thing?"

I was feeling very bad for all of us, but the thought of the police calling at Lenny's house was making me feel worse.

"I'll get it back," I said. "I'll go to his house. It's only along the road from the school. And if I don't get it back, I can get the exact number of where he lives. *Then* you can telephone the police." I had never spoken to my dad like that before, but I was feeling all shaky inside, and all the world seemed a different place to me that evening. I didn't give anybody a chance to argue with me. I ran straight out of the room and down to the street.

My secret hopes of seeing Lenny before I got to his house didn't come to anything. All too quickly I was there, pushing back his broken gate and walking up the cracked path to his front door. There wasn't a door knocker. I flapped the letter-box, and I started to think my dad was right. The police would have been better doing this than me.

I had never seen his mother before, only heard about her from other kids who lived near. When she opened the door, I could see she was a small lady with a tight mouth and eyes that said, "Who are you?" and "Go away from here!" at the same time.

She opened the door only a little bit, ready to slam it on me. I had to be quick.

"Is Lenny in, please?" I asked her.

She said, "What's it to you?"

"He's a friend of mine," I told her. "Can I see him, please?"

She made a face as if she had something nasty in her mouth. "LENNY!" she shouted. "COME HERE!"

Lenny came slinking down the passage, like one of those scared animals in a circus. He kept his eyes on her hands, once he'd seen who it was at the door. There weren't any funny remarks coming from him.

She jerked her head at me. "How many times have I told you not to bring kids to the house?" she shouted at him. She made it sound as if she was accusing him of a bad crime.

Lenny had nothing to say. She was hanging over him like a vulture about to fix its talons into a rabbit. It looked so out of place that it didn't seem real. Then it came to me that it could be play-acting – the two of them. He had given her the five pounds, and she was putting this on to get rid of me quickly.

But suddenly she slammed the door so hard in my face I could see how the glass in it came to be broken.

"Well I don't want kids coming to my door!" she shouted at him on the other side. "Breaking the gate, breaking the windows, wearing out the path. How can I keep this place nice when I'm forever dragging to the door?"

She hit him then, I know she did. There was no play-acting about the bang as a foot hit the door, and Lenny yelling out loud as if a desk lid had come down on his head. But I didn't stop to hear any more. I'd heard enough to turn my stomach sick. Poor Lenny – I'd been worried about my mum and dad seeing him – and look what happened when his mother saw me! She had to be mad, that woman. And Lenny had to live with her! I didn't feel like crying, although my eyes had a hot rawness in them. More than anything, I just wanted to be back at home with my own family and the door shut tight.

Seeing my dad's car turn the corner was as if my dearest wish had been granted. He was going slowly, searching for me, with Nalini sitting up in front with big eyes. I waved, and ran to them. I got in the back and I drew in my breath to tell them to go straight home. It was worth fifty pounds not to have them knocking at Lenny's house, never mind five. But they were too busy trying to speak to me.

"Have you been to the house? Did you say anything?"

"Yes, I've been to the house, but –"

"Did you accuse him?"

"No. I didn't have a chance –"

They both sat back in their seats, as if the car would drive itself home.

"Well, we must be grateful for that."

"We found the Postal Order."

I could hardly believe what my ears were hearing. *They had found the Postal Order.* Lenny hadn't taken it after all!

"It wasn't in its envelope," Nalini was saying. "He must have taken it out of that when he was tempted by it. But we

can't accuse him of screwing up an envelope and hiding it in his pocket."

"No, no," I was saying, urging her to get on with things and tell me. "So where was it?"

"In with the 'Monopoly' money. He couldn't put it back on the television, so he must have kept it in his pile of 'Monopoly' money, and put it back in the box."

"Oh."

"Mum found it. In all the commotion after you went out she knocked the box off the chair, and when she picked the bits up, there was the Postal Order."

"It's certainly a good job you said nothing about it," my dad said. "And a good job I didn't telephone the police. We should have looked very small."

All I could think was how small I had just felt, standing at Lenny's slammed door and hearing what his mother had said to him. And what about him getting beaten for having a friend call at his house?

My dad tried to be cheerful. "Anyway, who won?" he asked.

"Lenny won the 'Monopoly'", I said.

In bed that night, I lay awake a long time, thinking about it all. Lenny had taken some hard punishment from his mother. Some Red-Letter Day it had turned out to be! He would bear some hard thoughts about Prakash Patel.

He didn't come to school for a long time after that. But when he did, my heart sank into my boots. He came straight across the playground, the same flappy sleeves and dragging trouser bottoms, the same long, tangled hair – and he came straight for me. What would he do? Hit me? Spit in my face?

As he got closer, I saw what was on his shirt, pinned there like a medal. It was his birthday badge.

"It's a good game, that 'Monopoly'," he said out of the corner of his mouth. It was if he was trying to tell me something.

"Yes," I said. "It's a good game all right."

I hadn't got the guts to tell him that I'd gone straight home that night and thrown it in the dustbin. Dealings with houses didn't appeal to me any more.

The tale of the useful boy

It was bad enough being a girl and going out to work in service when I was young but it was much worse for boys. Not of course for boys in high-up situations – our mam's brother had gone in as a boots-and-knife boy to a Big House and ended up as a Lordship's Butler – but boys as went in as "Usefuls" in an ordinary household. They weren't trained for much, and when they got bigger and their appetites grew they were paid off and someone else took their place. Usually they were taken on for Charity.

There was a boy like that in the place next door to my Miss Johnson. The people who lived there had two of them joined-together surnames: Scott-Browning I think it was, though I might have misremembered. Anyway, they had a big house and garden with an apple-and-pear orchard between us and them. All the houses were built on the slope of a hill, and us being above them we could look over our garden wall right on to the orchard tree-tops.

These Scott-Brownings had a living-in girl too. She was about my age, a squatty dark thing called Ethel who was afraid of her shadow, and this boy, Mason they called him, who hardly lived-in because he bedded down in the mouldy hay on top of the stable where there used to be a horse. (Mr and Mrs Scott-Browning didn't have a horse, no more did my Miss Johnson: when they wanted to be driven anywhere they sent a note down to a cab rank by the station.)

When I first went to Miss Johnson's I thought I was in Heaven. I thought she was such a nice *old* dear – all of forty-five she must have been then – a deal younger than I am now, but I thought she was very ancient! Mind you, could I be blamed when ladies over forty dressed like Charlie's Aunties,

in blacks and dark browns and wore caps with lappets and mittens all day long?

She was sprightly too. Tended her little garden, and gave a real hand with the housework and talked to me as if I was as good as she was. She'd been a governess once and travelled overseas with her people. She told me a lot about foreign lands. She'd been to a place where the streets were water and people went up and down in long thin boats like we went in cabs and to somewhere where all the houses had been buried in cinders when a mountain had blowed up, that people had dug out again with all the bits and pieces of crockery and such; and plaster effigies of the people who'd burned there laid out like a poppy-show. Very interesting it all was.

Miss Johnson gave me a little brooch made out of tiny bits of coloured stones called mosaic and a painting called the Blue Grotto that she'd done herself when she was in foreign parts. She wanted to give me some reading and writing lessons too, but I dodged away from that. I said, "Please 'um, I think you'd just be wasting your time 'um – because I'm naturally *opaque*."

I didn't know what "opaque" meant, but I'd once heard a young gentleman telling a friend that someone was opaque when he meant muddle-headed – it was a slang word of the time I think. Miss Johnson laughed herself nearly sick about it and said well, if I was sure, she wouldn't worry me for she couldn't see any reason for hammering learning into happy heads that didn't need it. She said she'd done enough of that in her time. Thank heaven her auntie's money had made it so she didn't have to bother anymore!

Anyway – that's just to let you know how nice Miss Johnson was and give you an idea as to why I got so comfortable and at-home at her place, like we was real friends as well as people from different stations in life, and why when it came to helping that Mason next door when he was in trouble I turned to Miss Johnson.

At home we'd always been used to getting up early, so it was nothing for me to be around pegging out the mid-week wash at six o'clock of a summer's morning before me Miss was up. Sometimes, when I'd finished, I'd grab a crust of bread and butter and, holding it between me teeth, I'd shin up one of our fruit trees and sit on a branch and gnaw me vittles and look down a-top of all those green pears and apples in the Scott-Browningses' orchard. After that I might swing from me arms and drop down on to the path that was thick with moss; sometimes I'd lie on one of the broad branches with me legs up against the trunk, and rock meself and sing like a baby in its cradle or a dickeybird in its nest – showing me calico drawers and not caring because I thought there'd be no one around to see them.

That's how I came to speak to that Mason. For one morning I was just dropping down from me perch when I noticed that boy crouched low down under the orchard trees, gnawing away on a hard old green pear, and staring at me as if I was something strange the like of which he'd never seen before. This came as a shock, me thinking I had got the morning to meself, and knowing I had been behaving in a disrespectable way, I snapped at him sharp. "Well," I says, "Did you get your eyeful? Paid your tuppence?" which was the way girls snapped at the young chaps who whistled when they showed their ankles when they climbed up off the paddle-steamer on a Saturday over Hampton Court.

But this boy didn't give a sarky answer, he just went on staring and his eyes got all wet and swimmy with tears as if he couldn't bear another nasty word from anyone in the world. So, instead of berating him further, I leaned over our wall and looked down on him where he was crouching.

"You'll get belly-ache if you eat them green things," I says. "Ain't you had breakfast?" And he shook his head. "After they've ate," he tells me and nods towards his master's house. "I has what they leaves. I'm always hungry," he says.

Then he tells me his name was Mason and about sleeping in the stable and that. He wasn't sure how old he was and he thought his other name was Dick.

"What about the girl?" I asked him. "I've seen a girl

beating the carpet on them lines down there. Don't she give you anything?" Mason says no, sometimes that girl even eats some of his bits, she gets hungry too.

Now I had been in places where the food was pretty miserable and I'd been at Miss Ellum's where I'd gorged like a pig, but I'd never been given leavings. I knew if I had, our mam would have had me home quick.

I could see that Mason was as thin as a stick, and by his manner I could tell he was worried and frightened his Master and Missus would know he'd been complaining. He was afraid in case they sent him away, for in them days you might well starve to death without a job.

I said, "Well, cheer up, mate," and I told him how my Miss J. never minded how much I went into the loaf at mealtimes. "Look," I says, "I was going to butter myself another hunk with a dap of red jam to it, but instead, I'll give it to you if you like, so long as you promise not to tell a soul." That way he could feel he'd got a secret over me as well as me having one over him, though I knew my Miss wouldn't have cared a bit if she knew.

So I spread the hunk of bread and the boy stood against the wall below and I dropped it into his hands and he took it back away under the trees and that was the last I saw of him for that morning.

He was there again the next morning though. This time he was a bit luckier, for Miss Johnson had had an old dear's tea-fight the afternoon before – three of her friends from Mortlake – and there had been some sandwiches and a morsel of cake over. "Drop them in Mr Williamses' bucket next time you go down to the shop," she tells me, "There's not enough there to save, and anyway the bread would be hard by tomorrow."

Mr Williams was the pork butcher, and there was a big bucket with a lid in his side-alley for pig-bits. People often left scraps in it. I thought, "Well, that there Mason is a lot more deserving than pigs," so I hid up the scraps and saved them for his breakfast. He grabbed them like they were silver and gold and pelted off with them and that's all I saw of him that day.

The next morning he was there and so was that Ethel – both of them – all eyes like starving sparrows. After that, I gave them our scraps, and now and again I'd lay out a ha'penny bag of stales from the baker. In them days bakers used to sell off the day before's stale buns and things in the early morning before they opened shop. I'd let meself out dead early and be down by his yard-gate afore anyone else was stirring. I wonder now if he thought I was buying them for Miss J. because he used to give us some funny looks when we went by his shop.

The way them two kids ate! Once I left the porridge over the fire and it burned and Miss Johnson said to throw it away, and that Ethel and that Mason got through the whole lot.

Them Scott-Brownings were a fat old pair. Him especially – with one of them great big round fronts. On Sundays they had a job getting into church side-by-side they was so nourished-looking.

"I wonder you don't blow up at them," I says to Mason. "I'd want to upturn their dinners on their heads."

Mason had a dry little laugh. "*She* does things to them sometimes," he says and that Ethel nods.

"Spiders and beetles," says Mason, "mooshed up with a spoon and stirred into the hot-pot."

"I bet you put her up to it," I says, for I could see that Ethel was so beat and so squatty she'd never have thought of such an own-back as that.

But she must have been tough, that one, in spite of her low diet and the hard work – for apart from a cheap and drunken charwoman those two kids ran the housework – it was Mason who got frailer and frailer.

By winter he was light as a shadow and his face was all eyes, and he coughed and coughed. My little bedroom was within earshot of the Scott-Brownings' stables and I could hear him hacking and racking away, it was pitiful.

One November morning I crept out into the foggy darkness, with a shawl over me head and hands in mittens and whispered over the wall, and only that Ethel whispered back.

"Where's Mason then?" I says, and Ethel tells me he's been put off. "Missus says he's slacking off the work," she tells me. "They're going to get a girl instead, because girls is stronger."

"Where's he gone to?" I asks. It really upset me. Weather like what we were having, mists straight up from the river and a smack of frost to it.

"Dunno," that Ethel says. "He just took his bundle and went. He didn't half look bad at that."

Three mornings later Mason was under the wall again – dear knows where he had been in the meantime for he looked terrible. Some boys had pinched his bundle, and he hadn't eaten since he'd been turned off. He was shivering and quite wore out.

"I'm lying up at the stables for a bit," he whispers. "It was the only place I could think of. No one will know, they never goes there."

"Does Ethel know?" I asks. And he says, no, she's weak he says, "She'd be bound to let on to save herself in case they found out later."

"You go back then," I says, "And I'll find you something hot and I'll bring it as soon as I can."

After me Miss had had her breakfast I drained off the tea from the pot and warmed it up in a little saucepan with some sugar and a pinch of ginger like our mam did for fevers, and when it was ready I poured it into a tin can with a lid.

It wasn't easy for me to get down that wall with the drink and all, but I managed somehow. I found the track through the trees that led to the stables and I let myself in.

It wasn't half a dark old cobwebby ruin of a place and didn't it stink! I reckon it had been left just as it was when the last horse had been led out of it.

Mason had made a bed for himself up in the loft, all among the damp and mouldy hay. I couldn't hardly see him it was so dark. I felt for his face and it was as hot as fire. He drank the tea and almost at once he dropped off to sleep and when he slept his breath was raspy like an old, old man's.

I went back to our place by the roadway, through the Scott-Browning's side-gate and managed it without me Miss finding out. Ours was quite a small place – no more than a cottage really, but when Miss Johnson was in her little parlour with her fire and her books she never heard a thing. I slipped off two more times to take a look at poor Mason. Each time he seemed worse than before. He got light-headed and didn't know me, and then he cried to himself like a baby. It was awful to hear him going on so in the smelly old dark.

There was only one thing to do, and that was to tell Miss. So I did. I owned up to everything. The scraps that didn't get to Mr Williams' bucket and all.

"In the stable, in this weather?" Miss Johnson says. "Why didn't you tell me before, you silly, silly child? We must move him at once."

We wrapped ourselves up and went round to the Scott-Browningses there and then. Miss tatted on the door without stop till that Ethel opened it. She said her Master and Missus were out for the day and me Miss said, perhaps it was just as well, for she might not be able to keep her hands off them. She *was* in a state.

So then we went round to the stable – me, Miss J. and that scared Ethel, who was afraid of what her Missus would say, and afraid of Miss Johnson, and not too sure of me, either.

Poor Mason was rough-bad by now and he breathed all the time like he was choking. Miss sent that snivelling Ethel back to the house for blankets and a lamp, and me down to the High Street for one of the doctors. After he'd looked at poor Mason the doctor sent me back to the High Street again to fetch a policeman.

That Ethel just stood at the back saying, "Oh, what

will *they* say about the blankets. You'll tell them I didn't know he was here," – over and over till me Miss got mad with her and told her to hold her tongue, she was upsetting the boy.

There was only once place for Mason then, and that was Miss Johnson's cottage in the spare bedroom where her nice lady friends stayed when they made their genteel summer visits.

I got a fire going and Ethel warmed bricks in the oven for the bed. Then the constable carried poor Mason down the loft ladder and round the road to our place and Miss and the doctor got him in to bed. He was coughing and muttering and light-headed all the time.

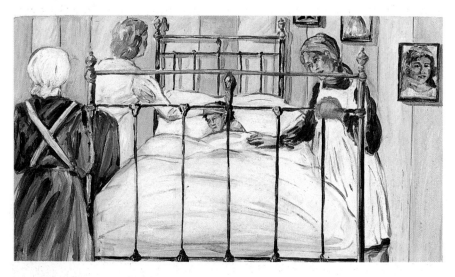

Ethel was so frightened she wouldn't go back to the big house to face her Master, so me Miss said she could stay the night with us. You should have seen the supper she ate! Mine as well as her own, for I was too upset to eat. She kept wondering what the Scott-Brownings would think when they got back to a cold house and no supper.

Gossip spreads like butter in hot weather! Next day ladies were in and out with jars of jelly and cups of broth, with ears a-flap and cries of outrage, and from what I could judge there wasn't much to choose between their behaviour and the way people acted down our way when there had been a scandalous happening. The Vicar came with a big gentleman in checked trousers who was in a rare old state of rage. He was a newspaper writer. He and the Vicar went in afterwards to see the Scott-Browningses. I don't know what was said, or how it came out in the papers, but it must have been hot, for those fat frauds moved from the district soon afterwards.

That Ethel got another post very quick with a dear old widow-lady who made a right pet of her. In fact, she was really spoiled and uppish in the end, and could hardly even nod at me when we met at the shops. Miss Johnson said people often acted that way towards folks who'd helped them. In the end she married and left our part of the world. I was glad none of my brothers had met and married her, when I think of those squashed beetles and things. Still, in fairness, it *was* Mason who'd put her up to that.

What about Mason? Well, it was sad really, but he was poor and unwanted and he'd never had enough nourishment inside him to fight back on. No. I woke up early with that Ethel snoring like a full pig beside me, and I crept across the landing to the spare bedroom, and there he was, and there *she* was: me nice Miss. She was fast asleep and holding his hand and him quite cold and dead – the poor little cock-sparrow.

Dick he thought his first name was. Dick Mason. And that's all anyone will ever know about him.

Well, you might think that's a very sad story to end up on, as sad as any of the Prize books me sister Aggie used to read aloud of a Sunday afternoon, the ones that are all about kind ladies reading the Bible to poor ragged children who take sickly and die and go to heaven.

My Miss Johnson was very cut up at the time. She cried and cried as if poor Mason had been a near relation instead of the like of what he was. So I told her, if them books was anything to go by, I reckoned Dick would have been took up by the angels straightaway for he'd been ragged and sickly enough, dear knows.

"He'll be all right," I tells her, "three hot meals a day and a nice white outfit and wings to get around with and no one to hustle him about." I went on and on laying it out to cheer her up and in the end she laughed a bit. She says, "Let's hope it's just as you say, for I expect that was his idea of heaven. He deserves it. He never harmed anyone, poor lamb."

Nor he did, except for giving Ethel that squashed beetle idea, and who knows they could well have been nourishing anyway for, do you know, that stuff that makes them iced cakes pink is made of red beetles? Miss Johnson told me so, and pink iced cakes are lovely. Yes, I reckon he's up there somewhere and all I hope is I won't be so bad that they shut the gate at me when my time comes.

My friends

I have four good friends around my flats,
We all live on the same estate.
Their names are George, Ibrahim, Nazia and Paul,
We are good friends.
George is a Chinese boy who likes to muck about,
But at the same time he's very quiet –
He's like a lion cub, quiet but playful.
Ibrahim is a Turkish boy who comes from Cyprus.
He's like a wildcat sometimes.
Nazia is a Mauritian, he comes from Mauritius.
He puts on an act like a tiger.
Paul is an English boy who looks cool,
He's like a panther, ready to pounce.
I am like a cat, quiet and happy.
Ibrahim and me are friends
Although he is Turkish and I am Greek,
We come from countries all around the world,
We make new links together like links on a chain,
We share together our happiness and pain.

Michael Xenofontos and Dean Coventry

FAKENHAM JUNIOR SCHOOL NEWSPAPER

The newspaper that's made by the school for the school

You have a friend...

My problem is that these girls at school are picking on me. They are 10 and in the last year of Junior school. I wouldn't exactly call it bullying because it isn't very bad like hitting or anything but I'm worried that one day it will get worse and I want to be able to handle it. They are just calling me names and pushing me around – every other day and so on.

Sometimes it really worries me because they threaten to hit me after a lesson. I hang around with friends but they can't do anything about it. It can get scary and people don't notice anything. The teachers said that bullying is not allowed at school?!

Bullying is very serious. If it is light at first it can get heavier later on. There are many different levels of bullying and different kinds. If someone picks on you this is bullying and it should be stopped now before it gets any further. If it was just a one-off and you just don't get on then that's a different matter. But this sounds to me that if they are let off now, they'll get even worse when they get older in High School. You didn't say why you think they are doing this. It doesn't really matter because they shouldn't. You should either tell one of your teachers or better still the head teacher – or get someone else to do it – like your parent/guardian.

Everyone, if you haven't already tried to get help – do it now, and remember you have a friend ....

Isolation

One thing I always wanted when I was at school was to be part of a group. I would have given almost anything to be a member of one of those giggling gangs of girls who always walked home together and whispered secrets to each other in the playground.

As my family never settled down in one place for very long and I went to more than twenty schools I never achieved this ambition. I was always an outsider, a curiosity who people might be friendly to, but who could never really become one of them.

I noticed though that I was never the only one who was left out. At least I could console myself that there was a reason for my being alone. As well as being permanently a "new girl" I was also very shy, which didn't help matters. But in every class I was in there would be one or even two others who never had any friends. There seemed to be no special thing that marked them out from the rest. If sometimes they were fat, spotty, mean or suffered from halitosis, so did plenty of girls who had lots of friends.

These other outsiders should by rights have been perfect companions for me, but it didn't work out like that. I always avoided them like the plague. After all, to have made friends with one of the unwanted would have tarred me with the same brush.

Outside school it was just as bad. I come from a family of five children, all close in age. You would think we could have been friends with each other. At least you would think so unless you come from a big family yourself. With us it was more like an undeclared state of war. I remember once when I was about eight we had just moved to another house. It was on an estate and all the kids there went about in gangs. Each gang had clearly defined territory which I didn't know about at first. One Sunday morning I went out for a ride on my bike with my brother Mick who's a bit older than I am. He was doing no hands which I was always scared to try so he was some way behind me. I rode round a corner and there was a gang of boys and girls playing further down the road. I tried to ride past them but they stopped me.

"You can't come round here."

"Course I can. You can't stop me." I could afford to be brave, knowing my brother would catch up any minute. The biggest boy came up. He was about my brother's size.

"Clear off or I'll bust your bike."

Just then, much to my relief, Mick came round the corner.

"You'd better watch it, that's my brother."

Mick rode up and got off his bike. The other boy sized him up.

"She says she's your sister."

"What of it?" said Mick. The boy smiled.

"Here, I want to talk to you a minute."

Mick and the boy stood whispering together, occasionally looking round at me. Two other boys were holding my handlebars so I couldn't get away. I didn't mind though. I knew Mick would make it all right.

Mick and the boy stopped talking and came over to me. I waited expectantly.

"All right, clear off," the boy said. I gave Mick a horrible look but he wouldn't look back at me. They turned my bike round with me still on it. I didn't even struggle. Mick's betrayal had completely stunned me. I felt very sorry for myself as I rode back. At the corner I stopped and looked round. I couldn't even make Mick out in the group. He had become indistinguishable from the rest. Suddenly a stone hit me in the chest. I couldn't be absolutely sure but just before I pedalled off as fast as I could go I thought I saw Mick's face and his hand up as if he had just thrown something. He swears to this day it wasn't him but I've never quite believed him.

As I got older I found the best thing to do was to pretend I had no friends simply because I didn't want any. When I went to new schools or new places to live I never tried to be friendly with anyone, however nice they were to me. That way I still didn't have any friends but at least I didn't risk people feeling sorry for me and instead of knowing I was shy they just thought I was cold and snooty.

I didn't know how good I had become at covering up my real feelings from other people until one day when I was sixteen. I was just starting, once again, a new school. It was the last term of the fifth form and as I was leaving at the end of it there was no point in my having a school uniform. My sister who was fourteen was starting with me. At least she had a uniform. I had on a blue polo-neck jumper and a grey skirt. They were much nicer than the dark-brown uniform but they made me more conspicuous which was the last thing I wanted. While the other girls were streaming into the school I stood casually chatting with my sister on the other side of the road. I knew I had to go in sometime but I was putting it off as long as possible.

The bell rang and everyone disappeared inside the school. My sister started to run. "Come on, we'll be late." We got as far as a low wall inside the playground and suddenly I panicked. I just couldn't go in. I got down behind the wall, shaking and crying. My sister got frightened too so we both just crouched there. It was only a low wall. We didn't know what to do. We couldn't go back because everyone would see us out of the windows and we didn't dare to go forward into the school.

The main door of the school opened and two women came out, obviously teachers. They were walking out of the school, across the playground and were bound to see us as they went past. I quickly dried my face and stood up as if I had been tying my shoes and my sister did the same.

We went into the school. After the effort of doing that it was quite easy to force myself to walk into the classroom in front of the sea of strange faces. I did it automatically like a

robot, my eyes unfocused so they wouldn't meet any strangers' eyes and give me away.

About a month after that it was raining at break so the girls stayed in the classroom. They were talking and I was reading so nobody would try to talk to me. I heard my name so I looked up. A girl with red hair who sat in front of me said, "I was just saying, I'd love to be as confident as you are. The way you walked in here that first day. You could tell you didn't give a damn, you just strolled in. I'd have been scared to death. You haven't got a nerve in your body, have you?"

I looked at her. In a way I would have liked to tell her the truth but I knew she wouldn't believe it if I did. It would just have been worth it to see her reaction.

Instead I shrugged. "That sort of thing doesn't bother me."

I went back to my reading.

The funny thing is that what started as an act became the truth. I am still shy of meeting people but I really don't want to have anything but the most casual relationship with them. I'll talk to them, I don't even mind them knowing how shy I am, but I have no desire to get to know them any better, I feel quite happy on my own.

You might think that's a bad attitude. I don't. After all, we're all on our own really. The man lying in the side of the road who everyone steps over so carefully without looking at him might be anything. He's probably drunk but what's the difference? One thing's for sure, nobody's going to stop and find out. He's on his own just like the rest of us.

The fieldmouse's monologue

Didn't you know how frightened I was when I came
For shelter in your room? I am not tame.
You looked enormous when I saw you first.
I rushed to the hole I had made, took refuge there,
Crouched behind paper you thrust at me, shivered with fear.
I had smelt some chocolate. The kitchen was warm below
And outside there was frost and, one whole night, great snow.

I only guessed you were frightened too when you
Called out loudly, deafeningly to me.
My ears are small but my hearing strong, you see.
You pushed old papers against my hole and so
I had to climb into a drawer. You did not know
That I could run so high. I felt your hand,
Like my world in shadow, shudder across me and
I scuttled away but felt a kind of bond
With you in your huge fear.
Was I the only friend near?

Elizabeth Jennings

Prince Llewellyn and the red-haired man

There is another tale told about Prince Llewellyn, and this is it. He was a devout man and loved to spend much time at Trefriw where he would offer up prayers to St Mary of that place. On one occasion he had been praying there before making a journey to see his father-in-law, King John, at his court in London.

He set out for the journey with a hundred of his men, and they had not gone far when they arrived at a place called Cefn Tegeingl. Coming towards them they saw a rough-looking man with red hair, ragged clothes and no shoes. Some of the men began to jeer at him, but the red-haired man took no notice of them and, walking up to Llewellyn's horse, he took hold of the bridle.

"Hey, what d'you think you're doing, eh?" shouted one of the Prince's men. "Take your dirty hands off the bridle of the Prince's horse."

"Let him be," said Prince Llewellyn; "he does no harm."

"Where are you going, sire," asked the man.

47

"Why, to London," replied the Prince.

"I should like to come with you if you will let me," said the man, and he seemed so eager the Prince had not the heart to refuse him.

"Come with us, and welcome," he said.

The red-haired man was given a horse and joined the other men. Quite soon the Prince forgot about him but, when they reached London and he was dismounting stiffly from his horse, the fellow came up to him again and said:

"Should there be anything you want of me, sire, send for me. I have certain magical powers that could be used to your advantage."

The Prince thanked him gravely, and they parted. Llewellyn went to King John's court and was made welcome there, although he was but a poor prince, and was not thought of highly in English court circles.

That night there was a banquet, and the King placed Llewellyn at the table of his son, Prince Henry. When the feast was at its end King John's wizard was called for to perform his wonderful feats for the company.

"Now you will see something that nothing in Wales can equal," whispered Prince Henry to Prince Llewellyn.

The King's wizard was an old man with a long white beard; he wore magnificent clothes of bright blue brocade that matched his piercing eyes, and decorating his cloak were the various signs of the zodiac in gold and silver. Raising his gnarled hand, he made a few movements in the air, and then it seemed as if the whole banqueting hall was full of the sea with ships sailing on it that carried fine merchandise, and these ships seemed to sail majestically past the astonished eyes of the company. With a wave of his other hand, the wizard caused the sea and the ships to vanish, and in their

place appeared a dirty yard about which ran goats, sheep and cattle, while pretty milkmaids milked the cows. The goats even ran along the tables; one passed right in front of Llewellyn.

"There," said one of the nobles, "is this not a remarkable wizard? I don't suppose you, being a mere prince of Wales, even possess a wizard, let alone one as clever as this."

These words angered Llewellyn, and he called one of his servants to his side.

"Go quickly," he said, "and fetch the red-haired man who travelled here with us from Trefriw. Tell him I have need of his services, and here is money that he may arrive dressed in better clothes."

But when the red-haired man was found, he refused the money for the clothes and arrived at the palace in his rags and barefooted as before.

"With your permission, your Majesty," said Llewellyn to King John, "I should like my wizard to show the company what he can do."

When the King, the princes, the nobles and the magnificently dressed English wizard saw this poor-looking ragged man, they laughed; but the King gave his permission all the same, out of politeness to his guest.

Nervously Llewellyn whispered to the red-haired one: "I hope that you are indeed as clever as you make out for I have little wish to be shamed in front of these English lords."

"Have no fear," said the red-haired wizard and, without more ado, he snapped his fingers and the sea again seemed to come into the banqueting hall, but this sea was of an incredible colour, neither blue nor green, but a mixture of both, and the ships that sailed on it were of silver and gold, their prows encrusted with precious jewels, and their merchandise of silks, spices and exotic fruits piled high in their bows for all to see.

Snapping his fingers again, the wizard made the sea and ships disappear, and in the middle of the hall a great oak appeared, its leafy branches throwing shadows over the dining tables, and its acorns falling to the floor where a herd of pigs appeared to eat them. Then twenty-four servants were conjured out of the air who began to chase away the pigs.

The King's wizard had watched this show of magic with a jealous heart, and now he said:

"This is but Welsh trickery, and not true magic at all."

Whereupon the red-haired man touched him with his wand and he turned into a buck. The twenty-four servants turned into twenty-four hounds who, leaping at the buck, instantly killed him.

The company were too amazed and startled to say anything, but Llewellyn said:

"You are a great wizard indeed."

Then the King spoke:

"We are deeply impressed by this exhibition: little did we think to see such wonders. I could wish though that my own wizard had not been taken from me in this fashion."

The red-haired wizard bowed low to the King, then he struck the body of the dead buck with his wand, and it turned back into the old man, alive and well, and none the worse for his adventure.

Llewellyn left the court in a blaze of glory, and was about to return to his humble lodgings in another part of London when the red-haired man stopped him, saying:

"My lord, your dwelling-place is not fit for a prince of Wales. Look, here is a palace for you."

And with a wave of his wand, he produced a wonderful palace right in front of them. And the Prince dwelt there in happiness and comfort for three months and a fortnight.

When the time came for Llewellyn to return to Wales, his palace was well known and admired, and many wealthy men tried to rent it from him, offering him enormous sums of money for it.

But the man of the red hair said:

"Do not accept their offers for I must take this palace away."

So Llewellyn refused every offer for it and, on the day of departure, the wizard drew his wand along the walls, and the palace was no longer there.

Back to Wales rode Llewellyn, his men and the red-haired wizard, until they came to the place Cefn Tegeingl, near Trefriw, where they had first met the ragged man.

"I must leave you now," he said to Llewellyn, "but I should like you to know that I am an angel sent to help you by Mary of Trefriw and to save you from shame at the court of King John. Continue to pray to St Mary, and she will guide and guard you."

That was the last Prince Llewellyn saw of his red-haired friend, but he never forgot him, and he remained devoted to St Mary of Trefriw for the rest of his life.

The incredible journey

In the cold hour before dawn, the bull terrier woke, then staggered painfully to his feet. He was trembling with cold and was extremely hungry and thirsty. He walked stiffly in the direction of the pool nearby, passing on his way the cat, who was crouched over something held between his paws. The terrier heard a crunching sound as the cat's jaws moved, and, wagging his tail in interest, moved over to investigate. The cat regarded him distantly, then stalked away, leaving the carcass; but to the terrier it was a disappointing mess of feathers only. He drank long and deeply at the pool and on his return tried the feathers again, for he was ravenous; but they stuck in his gullet and he retched them out. He nibbled at some stalks of grass, then, delicately, his lips rolled back over his teeth, picked a few overripe raspberries from a low bush. He had always liked to eat domestic raspberries this way, and although the taste was reassuringly familiar, it did nothing to appease his hunger. He was pleased to see the young dog appear presently; he wagged his tail and licked the other's face, then followed resignedly when a move was made towards the direction of the road. They were followed a few moments later by the cat, who was still licking his lips after his feathery breakfast.

In the grey light of dawn the trio continued down the side of the road until they reached a point where it took a right-angled turn. Here they hesitated before a disused logging trail that led westward from the side of the road, its entrance almost concealed by overhanging branches. The leader lifted his head and appeared almost as though he were searching for the scent of something, some reassurance; and apparently he found it, for he led his companions up the trail between the overhanging trees. The going here was softer; the middle was overgrown with grass and the ruts on either side were full of dead leaves. The close-growing trees which almost met overhead would afford more shade when the sun rose higher. These were all considerations that the old dog needed, for he had been tired today even before he started, and his pace was already considerably slower.

Both dogs were very hungry and watched enviously when the cat caught and killed a chipmunk while they were resting by a stream in the middle of the day. But when the old dog advanced with a hopeful wag of his tail, the cat, growling, retreated into the bushes with his prey. Puzzled and disappointed, the terrier sat listening to the crunching sounds inside the bushes, saliva running from his mouth.

A few minutes later the cat emerged and sat down, daintily cleaning his whiskers. The old dog licked the black Siamese face with his panting tongue and was affectionately patted on the nose in return. Restless with hunger, he wandered up the banks of the creek, investigating every rock and hollow, pushing his hopeful nose through tunnels of withered sedge and into the yielding earth of molehills. Sadly he lay down by an unrewarding blueberry bush, drew his paws down tightly over his blackened face, then licked the dirt off them.

The young dog, too, was hungry; but he would have to be on the verge of starvation before the barriers of deep-rooted Labrador heredity would be broken down. For generations his ancestors had been bred to retrieve without harming, and there was nothing of the hunter in his make-up; as yet, any killing was abhorrent to him. He drank deeply at the stream and urged his companions on.

The trail ran high over the crest of this hilly, wooded country, and the surrounding countryside below was filled with an overwhelming beauty of colour; the reds and vermilions of the occasional maples; pale birch, and yellow poplar, and here and there the scarlet clusters of mountain ash berries against a rich dark-green background of spruce and pine and cedar.

Several times they passed log ramps built into the side of the hill, picking their way across the deep ruts left by the timber sleighs below; and sometimes they passed derelict buildings in rank, overgrown clearings, old stables for the bush horses and living quarters for the men who had worked there a generation ago. The windows were broken and sagging and weeds were growing up between the floorboards, and one old rusted cookstove even had fireweed springing from the firebox. The animals, strangely enough, did not like these evidences of human occupation and skirted them as far as possible, hair raised along their backs.

Late in the afternoon the old dog's pace had slowed down to a stumbling walk, and it seemed as if only sheer determination were keeping him on his feet at all. He was dizzy and swaying, and his heart was pounding. The cat must have sensed this general failing, for he now walked steadily beside the dogs, very close to his tottering old friend, and muttered plaintive worried bleats. Finally, the old dog came to a standstill by a deep rut half-filled with muddy water. He stood there as if he had not even the strength to step around it; his head sagged, and his whole body was trembling. Then, as he tried to lap the water, his legs seemed to crumple under him and he collapsed, half in and half out of the rut. His eyes were closed, and his body moved only to the long, shallow, shuddering breaths that came at widening intervals. Soon he lay completely limp and still. The young dog became frantic now: he whined as he scratched at the edge of the rut, then nudged and pushed with his nose, doing everything in his power to rouse the huddled, unresponsive body. Again and again he barked, and the cat growled softly and continuously, walking back and forth and rubbing his whole length against the dirty, muddied head. There was no response to their attention. The old dog lay unconscious and remote.

The two animals grew silent, and sat by his side, disturbed and uneasy; until at last they turned and left him, neither looking back – the Labrador disappearing into the bushes where the crack of broken branches marked his progress farther and farther away; the cat stalking a partridge which had appeared at the side of the trail some hundred yards away and was pecking unconcernedly at the sandy dirt. But at the shrill warning of a squirrel, it flew off across the trail with a sudden whirr into the trees, while the cat was still some distance away. Undaunted, still licking his lips in anticipation, the cat continued around a bend in the trail in search of another, and was lost to sight.

The shadows lengthened across the deserted track, and the evening wind sighed down it to sweep a flurry of whispering leaves across the rut, their brown brittleness light as a benison as they drifted across the unheeding white form. The curious squirrel peered in bright-eyed wonder from a nearby tree, clucking softly to itself. A shrew ran halfway across, paused and ran back; and there was a soft sound of wings as a whisky-jack landed and swayed to and fro on a birch branch, tilting his head to one side as he looked down and called to his mate to come and join him. The wind died away – a sudden hush descended.

Suddenly there was a sound of a heavy body pushing through the undergrowth, accompanied by a sharp cracking of branches, and the spell was broken. Chattering shrilly in alarm and excitement, the squirrel ran up the trunk of the tree and the whisky-jacks flew off. Now on to the trail on all fours scampered a half-grown bear cub, round furry ears pricked and small deep-set eyes alight with curiosity in the sharp little face as he beheld the old dog. There was a grunting snuffling sound in the bush behind the cub: his mother was investigating a rotten tree stump. The cub stood for a moment and then, hesitantly, advanced towards the rut where the terrier lay. He sniffed around, wrinkling his facile nose at the unfamiliar smell, then reached out a long curved black paw and tapped the white head. For a moment the mists of unconsciousness cleared, and the old dog opened his eyes, aware of danger. The cub sprang back in alarm and watched from a safe distance. Seeing that there was no further

movement, he loped back and cuffed again with his paw, this time harder, and watched for a response. Only enough strength was left in the old dog for a valiant baring of his teeth. He snarled faintly with pain and hatred when his shoulder was raked by the wicked claw of the excited cub, and made an attempt to struggle to his feet. The smell of the drawn blood excited the cub further; he straddled the dog's body and started to play with the long white tail, nibbling at the end like a child with a new toy. But there was no response: all conscious effort drained, the old dog no longer felt any pain or indignity. He lay as though asleep, his eyes veiled and unseeing, his lip still curled in a snarl.

Around the bend in the trail, dragging a large dead partridge by the wing, came the cat. The wing sprang back softly from his mouth as he gazed transfixed at the scene before him. In one split second a terrible transformation took place; his blue eyes glittered hugely and evilly in the black masked face, and every hair on the wheat-coloured body stood upright so that he appeared twice his real size; even the chocolate-coloured tail puffed up as it switched from side to side. He crouched low to the ground, tensed and ready, and uttered a high, ear-splitting scream; and, as the startled cub turned, the cat sprang.

He landed on the back of the dark furred neck, clinging with his monkeylike hind legs while he raked his claws across the cub's eyes. Again and again he raked with the terrible talons, hissing and spitting in murderous devilry until the cub was screaming in pain and fear, blinded with blood, making ineffectual brushing movements with his paws to dislodge the unseen horror on his back. His screams were answered by a thunderous roar as the huge black she-bear crashed through the bushes and rushed to the cub. She swiped at the clinging cat with a tremendous paw; but the cat was too quick for her and with a hiss of fury leaped to the ground and disappeared behind a tree. The unfortunate cub's head received the full force of the blow and he was sent spinning across the track into the bushes. In a blind, frustrated rage, maddened by the cries of her cub, the mother turned for something on which to vent her fury, and saw the still figure of the old dog. Even as she lumbered snarling towards him the cat distracted her attention with a sudden leap to the side of the track. The bear halted, then reared up to full height for attack, red eyes glinting savagely, neck upstretched and head weaving from side to side in a menacing, snake-like way. The cat uttered another banshee scream and stepped forward with a stiff-legged, sideways movement, his squinting, terrible eyes fixed on his enormous adversary. Something like fear or indecision crept into the bear's eyes as the cat advanced; she shuffled back a step with lowered head. Slow, deliberate, purposeful, the cat came on – again the bear retreated, bewildered by the tactics of this terrible small animal, distraught by her cub's whimpering, slowly falling back before the relentless inch-by-inch advance. Now the cat stopped and crouched low, lashing his tail from side to side – the bear stopped too, shifting her weight uneasily before the spring that must follow, longing to decamp but afraid to turn her back. A sudden crackle of undergrowth turned the huge animal into a statue, rigid with apprehension – and when a great dog sprang out of the bush and stood beside the cat, teeth bared and snarling, every hair on his russet back and ruff erect, she dropped to all fours, turned swiftly and fled towards her cub.

There was a last growl of desperate bravado from the bush and a whimpering cry; then the sounds of the bears' escape receded in the distance. Finally all was quiet again; the curious squirrel leaped from his ringside seat and scrambled farther down the trunk of the tree.

The cat shrank back to his normal size. His eyes regained their usual cool, detached look. He shook each paw distastefully in turn, glanced briefly at the limp, muddied bundle by his feet, blood oozing from four deep parallel gashes on the shoulder, then turned and sauntered slowly down the track towards his partridge.

The young dog nosed his friend all over, his lips wrinkling at the rank bear smell, then attempted to stanch the wounds with his rough tongue. He scratched fresh leaves over the bloodstained ones, then barked by the old dog's head; but there was no response, and at last he lay down panting on the grass. His eyes were uneasy and watchful, the hairs still stood upright in a ridge on his back, and from time to time he whined in perplexity. He watched the cat drag a large grey bird almost up to the nose of the unconscious dog, then slowly and deliberately begin to tear at the bird's flesh. He growled softly, but the cat ignored him and continued his tearing and eating. Presently; the enticing smell of raw, warm meat filtered through into the old dog's senses. He opened one eye and gave an appreciative sniff. The effect was galvanizing: his muddied half-chewed tail stirred and he raised his shoulders, then his forelegs, with a convulsive effort, like an old work horse getting up after a fall.

He was a pitiful sight – the half of his body that had lain in the rut was black and soaking, while the other was streaked and stained with blood. He looked like some grotesque harlequin. He trembled violently and uncontrollably throughout the length of his body, but in the sunken depths of the slanted black-currant eyes there was a faint gleam of interest – which increased as he pushed his nose into the still-warm bundle of soft grey feathers. This time there was no growling rebuff over the prey: instead the cat sat down a few yards away, studiedly aloof and indifferent, then painstakingly washed down the length of his tail. When the end twitched he pinned it down with a paw.

The old dog ate, crunching the bones ravenously with his blunt teeth. Even as his companions watched him, a miraculous strength slowly seeped back into his body. He dozed for a while, a feather hanging from his mouth, then woke again to finish the last morsel. By nightfall he was able to walk over the soft grass at the side of the track, where he lay down and blinked happily at his companions, wagging his pitiful tail. The Labrador lay down beside him, and licked the wounded shoulder.

An hour or two later the purring cat joined them, carelessly dropping another succulent morsel by his old friend's nose. This was a deer mouse, a little creature with big eyes and long hind legs like a miniature kangaroo. It was swallowed with a satisfying gulp, and soon the old dog slept.

But the cat purring against his chest and the young dog curled at his back were wakeful and alert most of the remaining night; neither moved from his side.

Aggie and Zoe

Zoe English and Agniescka Burza first met at junior school. They are no longer in the same class but they have stayed friends.

AGGIE: I'm Polish. I met Zoe when I came to England. I didn't know any English. Zoe was one of my very first friends. I was in her class for nearly as long as I can remember. She was one of the many people who all wanted to be friends with a foreign girl. I think when I was younger there wasn't all this argument about who was whose best friend.
"Oh, you like her better than me." I hate it.
Friends aren't friends if they can't share. If my two friends and I are talking and suddenly the two of them go off, I let them because I don't want to break up a friendship – that's the worst thing, because then I'd lose both friends... I have two best friends really – but it always depends on the circumstances – one at school who's in my class and one at home who lives close by me.

ZOE: I wanted to be friendly with
     Aggie because I didn't want her
     to be on her own without
     anybody in a new country. But
     I already had a best friend.
     My best friend I can really
     trust. She won't tell any of
     my secrets. I think we're
     quite like each other, we've
     got lots in common. We
     like the same, we do the same.

AGGIE: I've never found a friend who's kept every
     single one of my secrets. Probably the only person who will
     be all the things I want will be a husband later on. I
     couldn't trust any of my friends fully – but I can't really
     trust myself either! Keeping secrets doesn't bother me as
     long as friends aren't hypocritical, or hang around me all
     the time. People say you should stay with one friend all the
     time but I don't. For instance, if a friend wants to talk all
     the way through lessons I'm thinking, "shut up, shut up,
     shut up..."

     I like my own space. There's one friend who keeps on
     calling me up and wanting to do things because she's bored
     at weekends, but I don't want to, weekends are when I
     relax. Sometimes friends say you're not spending enough
     time with them – but if they can't take the fact that I want
     to be with other people that's just tough for them. They
     don't own me.

ZOE: Sometimes you want to be with your friend but
     something else is pulling you in a different direction. We've
     changed so much really. When I was little I wanted to be
     an astronaut! I don't like the idea at all now. I think Aggie

and I are quite alike as friends but different too, like half and half... Aggie's a bit sort of wimpish. For instance if we're on computers, I would press a button I didn't know anything about but Aggie would say "No, no! Don't do that, something might happen." I take the risks and Aggie plays safe.

We both love reading and like the same books and lend them to each other. We're friends at home too. Our families know each other because they go to the same church but they're very different from each other.

AGGIE: My sister doesn't like any of my friends. She tries to sabotage my friendships.

ZOE: My brother's like that. Whenever I have friends round he always shows off. He comes into my room when we're talking and says things in front of my friends. Parents sometimes do that too.

I think we've stayed friends because we don't see each other too much. The more you see each other, the more annoying people get... I'd see what they were really like and start going off them. That's how we get to bear each other, because we're not together in lessons all the time.

AGGIE: We share a sense of humour. But our choice of clothes is different. I'm all grey and black...

ZOE: I like wearing lots of bright colours...

AGGIE: So when we walk down the street I look as if I'm in mourning and she looks as if she's in a circus.

I don't like friends who are exactly the same as me... I look at them and I think, "Oh no ... am I really like that?" I don't like friends who try to copy me.

ZOE: I don't like friends trying to tie you down. If you don't answer a question the way they want, they go stomping off...

AGGIE: I think you're being a bit hypocritical, Zoe! I can think of lots of times when you did that...

ZOE: I don't do it any more!

AGGIE: Sometimes we've let each other down. One time I took a friend with me to Poland when I went back on holiday – and it was Zoe's worst enemy.

ZOE: And she never told me. We were meant to be doing a play together and I had to find someone else in about a day.

AGGIE: But the reason for that was that I thought you'd go storming off!

ZOE: Jealous ... yes. But I'm growing up a bit more now and don't do so much storming off.

AGGIE: The thing that annoys me most about Zoe is her openness about everything.

ZOE: Oh yeah! Like when Aggie came to school one day wearing this really short skirt and I said: "You look terrible, you must be freezing!"

AGGIE: She's never afraid to say I look horrible. I suppose it can be an asset in one way! But if you want to keep friends with someone I wouldn't advise you to say too much...

ZOE: The thing that annoys me about Aggie is that she talks too much. Probably three quarters of this interview is Aggie!

A recipe for friendship tea

A friend is like a slice of cake.
To bake her you will need to take
A tin of love
A reliable dove
A pinch of trust
And faith is a must.
Warm it up with good company
And serve it up with friendship tea.

Jodi Bamber

Friends on the Internet

The Internet is a network of computers throughout the world linked by telephone lines. Instead of sending letters through the post, you can type a message into a computer and send it instantly through the Internet.

To: ARIANA @ ROBINS ELEMENTARY SCHOOL

Hello,

My name is Sadie. I live in Sandford in England. I have got lots of pets including dogs and cats. I have got one sister called Leah and a mum and dad. The school I go to is Sandford Primary School. There are 120 children in it. The school was built in 1891. It is quite a small school with only 4 classes.

The school house is the biggest building in the school. This is where the head teacher used to live but now it is the school office, library and staff room. There is also a kitchen where children often cook things.

Our village is built on the edge of the Mendip Hills. There are the remains of iron-age hill forts all around. Bristol is the biggest city we live near. It is always busy and noisy there. We have also got Bath nearby. This was where the Romans built their baths over a hot spring. You can still visit them.
From Sadie.

Dear Sadie,

Hi! My name is Ariana. I live in Tucson, Arizona, USA. I have a mom and a dad and a sister (her name is Cayla). I have 2 dogs. One is named Tash and one is named Chaco. What kind of animals do you have? I go to Robins Elementary School. I have blonde hair and blue eyes. I like country music like Neil Young. What kind of music do you like? I can play the violin. I am in 4th grade.

Tucson is a neat place to live. It has a certain kind of tree called a cactus. Tucson is famous for its saguaro cactus, the most common cactus you see. Tucson also has lots of plants and animals. Coyotes are not a rare sight, neither are jackrabbits or hares. It is true Tucson does not have a whole lot of water, unlike Sandford. Even though we don't have a lot of water, we have enough water to quench the thirst of Tucson. Tucson is a town with about 500,000 people in it.

Thanksgiving is coming up. Do you celebrate Thanksgiving? I do. Some of my relatives are coming for Thanksgiving too. When Thanksgiving comes I always think about when the Pilgrims first came to North America. I am glad they started a town that after millions of years became North America.

I am happy to be key-pals with someone in another country.

Your key-pal,
Ariana.

Dear Ariana,

Thank you for writing to me. Your letter was very interesting.

I have got lots of pets including my pony called Mouse, two dogs, a rabbit and six cats. My sister Leah has also got some pets and my mum keeps chickens and ducks.

I have got light brown hair and grey eyes. I like most kinds of music. I do not play any musical instrument.

Sandford is a nice quiet village which is by the Mendip Hills. We get lots of animals, plants and trees including foxes, badgers and hedgehogs. During the summer we get flowers like roses.

The weather here now is wet and cold.
We celebrate Christmas and give each other gifts.
I am pleased to be your key-pal.
From Sadie.

Dear Sadie,

Thank you for answering my questions. You really surprised me! You are so lucky! You have tons of pets! You even have a horse! In Tucson most people don't have a horse. So as you can see, to me, you are very lucky.

Christmas is coming. What are you getting your parents? I don't know yet. Do you? Tonight we are putting up our tree. Do you put up a tree? My dad and mom put up lights all over our house. They look pretty. Please write back.

Sincerely,
Ariana.

Birthday boy

At the start of World War II in 1939, Willie is evacuated from London and goes to live with Tom Oakley, an elderly, unsociable man, and his dog, Sammy. Gradually Tom and Willie begin to make friends.

Willie leapt out of bed. Sammy was yapping and jumping up and down, waiting for him.

"Mornin'," said Tom, appearing at the back door. "Happy Birthday!" He expected Willie to ask if there had been any post but there was no response.

They had decided that every day Willie would practise writing and reading before leaving for school. When he had finished his chores he sat down at the table and copied out "I am William Beech" over and over again until Tom, after much effort, finally persuaded him to go for a run and exercise Sammy. He had only just disappeared down the graveyard path and out of sight when the postman arrived at the back gate.

"Anything from London?" asked Tom.

Matthew shook his head. "'Fraid not. I got parcels though and cards and this." It was a basket with fresh eggs, a newly-baked loaf of bread, a pat of butter and some rashers of bacon inside. "'Tis a birthdee breakfast from the Padfields."

Tom took the cards and parcels, together with the basket, indoors. It was a shame that there was nothing from the boy's mother, but then it was only Thursday and perhaps since war had been declared the post was being delayed.

Willie returned flushed and breathless, followed by Sammy. He flung the door open and was about to say something when he caught sight of the table.

On top of a red-and-white checkered tablecloth were two of the best plates, cups and saucers. In the centre stood a jam jar with flowers in it and surrounding Willie's place were two parcels and envelopes.

"Happy birthdee," said Tom.

"Are they fer me?" he asked in astonishment.

"'Tis where you usually sit, ent it? Go on, open them. I'll read out who they're from."

Willie picked up a soft brown-paper package and with trembling fingers slowly untied the string. Inside lay a green woollen balaclava, a green sleeveless pullover and a pair of navy blue shorts.

"Like to try them on?" said Tom.

Willie climbed out of his thin grey ones and stepped into the navy pair. The shorts were a little loose around the waist.

"Soon fill out, though," said Tom. He put the pullover on over Willie's shirt. "Stand back and let's have a look at you."

The top was also a little long, but not so that it looked foolish. The shorts hung comfortably down to the base of his knees. He beamed.

"Feel good, do they?"

"Yeh, they got pockets, too," he said, plunging his hands deep into them. He glanced at the balaclava. "Wot's that?"

"'Tis a balaclava. Keeps yer head and ears warm when the wind's nippy."

"Can I put it on now?"

"If you want."

"Who give it me?" he asked as he pulled it over his head.

"I did, but Mrs Fletcher made it."

"Ta," said Willie gratefully and he touched the soft wool of the pullover.

"Ent you goin' to open the rest?"

The next parcel contained some Chiliprufe underwear from May Thorne, who Willie had never even met. Emilia, her sister, had given him an illustrated copy of *The Wind in the Willows*. Inside she had written "To William on his ninth birthday. For Mr Oakley to read to you until you can read it yourself."

Willie held it tightly to his chest. "Is it fer me to keep?"

Tom nodded.

His own book. His very own book. The pages were crisp and white and were filled with the most marvellous pictures of animals wearing clothes. He placed the book carefully to one side and continued to open the other parcels. There was a white china egg-cup with a golf rim from Connie and Walter Bird, a boy's comic annual with lots of pictures and games in it from Doctor and Nancy Little, and a game of snap from the vicar and his wife. In addition to the parcels were seven birthday cards.

Willie was completely overcome. He sat down and stared at the gifts, quite speechless. Tom, meanwhile, took a large parcel out of the cupboard and placed it in front of him.

"That's me present from me to you."

"But you give me this," he said, indicating his pullover, "and these shorts."

"This is something different like."

Willie unwrapped the parcel and gave a start. There, before his eyes, lay one large and one small sketch pad. Pages and pages of untouched paper. There were two paintbrushes and three pots of paint. One brush was a medium-sized one, the other was thin and delicate. The paints were red, yellow and blue.

"If you mix them," said Tom, "you can also git orange, green and brown."

Wrapped up in tissue paper were a pencil, a rubber and a sharpener. Something was carved at the end of the pencil. It looked familiar. He traced it slowly with his finger. "William Beech."

He looked lovingly at the paints and brushes and swallowed a pain that had risen at the back of his throat.

"I take it you like them," murmured Tom. "I chose them meself, like."

"Thanks, Mister Tom," said Willie huskily. "I'll look after them real proper."

After a birthday egg-and-bacon fry up, Willie ran off to school. Tom met him outside at lunchtime as there were no classes for him in the afternoon. They visited the people who had given him presents so that he could thank them personally. It would save the agony of trying to write letters and Tom thought it would be a good opportunity for Willie to meet them. As for Tom, everyone was very surprised to see him, for he rarely visited anyone.

They strolled back home down the tunnelled lane and called in at the Little's cottage and the Vicarage on the way. Willie had looked around for the twins and George, but they were nowhere to be seen. Even at the Littles' there was no sight of Zach.

"P'rhaps they've gone blackberryin' " he thought and for a fleeting moment he wished that he was with them.

"How about stayin' outside this afternoon?" suggested Tom suddenly. "It's a fine day." His words were immediately contradicted by the appearance of a dark shadow across the sky. "Drat them blimmin' clouds," he muttered. Before they had reached the back gate a few drops of rain had already plopped warningly on their heads.

"I'll have to draw inside," said Willie to himself.

Tom grunted and then suddenly hit on an idea. "How about the church?" he exclaimed. "Of course, you could draw in there."

"Yeh," agreed Willie. "Yeh, I could."

He wrapped his mackintosh carefully round the small sketch-pad and fled down the pathway to the church, arriving in the nick of time, for as he closed the heavy arched door behind him, a slow drizzle of rain swept across the village and surrounding fields.

He stood quite still for a moment. It felt odd to be alone in a church. He stared up at the windows and then caught sight of the pulpit. Slinging his mac over the back of a pew he sat down and rested his feet on the one in front. He placed the sketch-pad on his knees, flicked open the first page and began to draw.

He didn't hear the rain suddenly stop. He was conscious only of the pulpit and his sketch-pad. The rest of the church had ceased to exist for him. Neither did he hear Zach repeatedly calling him from outside or the sound of his footsteps running up the tiny pathway to the back door.

The door opened slowly and Zach peeped in. He was just about to speak when he became aware that Willie was absorbed in some task. He took a few paces forward and leaned over Willie's small thin shoulders. His shadow fell across the pad. Willie jumped and turned round hurriedly placing his arm over the picture, but it was too late. Zach had already seen it.

"I say," he gasped, full of admiration, "that's magnificent."

Willie shyly flapped the cover of the pad over the drawing.

"You must show the..." but he checked himself. "Didn't you hear me call you. I practically tore my throat out yelling for you."

Willie shook his head.

"Er..." said Zach thoughtfully, feeling a little stumped for words, "Er, Mr Oakley says that he'd like to er... converse with you. Er... talk about the time of day. That sort of thing. He's waiting for you now."

"Is he?" said Willie in surprise and he picked up his mackintosh. "Is it still rainin'?"

"It finished an age ago," groaned Zach. "Hurry up or the ..." he stopped. "Er ... or ... it might start again."

They walked down the path towards the front door. He heard Sammy give an excited bark from the front room and then it immediately sounded muffled. Odd, thought Willie, but he shrugged it off and hung his mackintosh on his peg.

"Oh, do hurry," said Zach who was standing waiting at the door. Willie looked at him.

"Wot you waitin' for?" he asked.

"You go in first," and with that Zach pushed open the door and immediately the whole room erupted into:

"Happy Birthday to you,

Happy Birthday to you,

Happy Birthday, dear William,

Happy Birthday to you."

The twins, George, their mothers, Lucy and her mother and Tom were all standing in the front room singing, while Sammy sat in the middle and howled.

A large banner with "Happy Birthday William" on it hung above and across the range.

On the table stood two jellies, one red and one green. There was a plate of chocolate wafers, a plate of potted meat and fishpaste sandwiches and a plate of fairy cakes. In the centre of the table was an iced cake with nine lighted candles on it.

Zach was the first to break the ensuing silence.

"Was it a surprise?" he burst out. "Was it a real surprise? Did you guess?"

It was obvious from Willie's astounded expression that he had no idea at all.

So this was what a birthday party was like. He had heard people at school talking about them. He looked towards Tom for help.

"You gotta blow the candles out, boy."

"And if you manage to blow them all out at once you can make a wish," said Carrie.

Willie leaned over, took a deep breath and blew. Six candles went out the first time, the remaining three the second time. Everyone applauded.

"You can still have a wish," said Zach, "when you cut the cake, only you mustn't talk till after you've made it and it must remain a secret else it won't come true and..."

"We'll be 'ere till doomsday if you go bletherin' on," said Tom.

Willie held the knife above the cake, screwed up his face till he had thought of a wish and then plunged the knife into the icing.

They had just sat down when Zach suddenly let out a cry.

"I nearly forgot. You haven't seen Will's picture."

Willie was still holding his sketch-pad tightly under his arm. His face turned pink.

"You drawn a picture?" asked Tom.

"Can we see it?" said Carrie.

"Please," added Ginnie.

He lifted the cover up shyly. George came and stood by his side and gave a low whistle.

"I told you, didn't I?" said Zach.

Tom leaned over their heads and peered down. It was a copy of the carved eagle on the pulpit. Its strong stubborn wings were swept back in a magnificent curve. Around it Willie had added rain so that it appeared to be flying against a great wind.

"That's a find hand you have there, William," said Tom quietly. "A fine hand."

Willie blushed crimson.

They all settled down to eating while Willie, amidst all the chatter and laughter, found himself an object of praise. After tea, there were more presents. A jigsaw from the twins, coloured pencils from Zach, sweets from George and some small cakes from Lucy.

"She baked them herself," said her mother.

"Ta," he said awkwardly, and she gave him one of her voluminous smiles.

After playing several party games, everyone finally returned home. Tom and Willie stood outside and watched them leaving. They turned back into the sitting room and closed the door.

"Mister Tom," said Willie touching his sleeve. "It's the best ... it's the best," but he never finished. The excitement and food simply welled up inside him and he gave a short gasp and vomited all over the carpet.

A dream

I say
Open our hearts
Like a new flower

Let the hatred in us
flow away like a stream
Let Justice be set in our hearts
Like a stone standing
Straight and firm

I have a dream that one day
people all around the world
shall eat from the plate of peace
and say together
"We shall stay so always."

One day
a tree will grow high and strong
in the garden of Justice

And live forever

Tabassum Khan